I Just want to Do It
MY WAY!

Written by
Julia Cook

Illustrated by
Kelsey De Weerd

BOYS TOWN
Press

Boys Town, Nebraska

To Cart – My BEST friend!

I Just Want to Do It My Way!

Text and Illustrations Copyright © 2013, by Father Flanagan's Boys' Home
ISBN 978-1-934490-43-3

Published by the Boys Town Press
14100 Crawford St.
Boys Town, NE 68010

For a Boys Town Press catalog, call **1-800-282-6657**
or visit our website: **BoysTownPress.org**

Publisher's Cataloging-in-Publication Data

Cook, Julia, 1964-

I just want to do it my way! : my story about staying on task and asking for help! / written by Julia Cook ; illustrated by Kelsey De Weerd. -- Boys Town, NE : Boys Town Press, c2013.

p. ; cm.
(Best me I can be ; 5th)

ISBN: 978-1-934490-43-3

Audience: grades K-6.
Summary: RJ's way of doing things isn't working out for him. His teacher is upset because so many of his assignments are missing or incomplete, but RJ blames other students for distracting him. He learns how to ask for help and stay on task, and discovers that by doing things the right way the first time, he no longer has to do them over and over again.

1. Children--Life skills guides--Juvenile fiction. 2. Distraction (Psychology)--Juvenile fiction. 3. Attention in children--Juvenile fiction. 4. Help-seeking behavior--Juvenile fiction. 5. Children's audiobooks. 6. [Success--Fiction. 7. Attention--Fiction. 8. Problem-solving--Fiction. 9. Helpfulness--Fiction. 10. Thought and thinking--Fiction.] I. De Weerd, Kelsey. II. Series: Best me I can be (Boys Town) ; no. 5.

PZ7.C76984 I18 2013

E   1301

Printed in the United States
10 9 8 7 6 5 4 3 2 1

Boys Town Press is the publishing division of Boys Town, a national organization serving children and families.

My name is RJ,
and I have my own way
of doing things.

3

I sleep with my pajamas on
inside out every Friday night.

I put on both my shoes first,
and then I tie them.

I eat ice cream cones from the
bottom up, even though it's messy.

And, I always save my math homework for last because I don't like doing math AT ALL!

Last week, my teacher called my mom and told her I have a hard time staying on task... especially during math time. She also told her that I have seven math papers that I haven't handed in.

"RJ, where are your math assignments?" my mom asked me.

"Oh, they're in my desk at school," I said.

"Why didn't you hand them in?"

"Well, I kinda sorta didn't quite get them all the way finished."

"I don't like to do math. It's really hard on me!
When my answer is six, the right answer's three.

I'd much rather do anything other than math.
I'd rather eat parsnips, or even take a bath!

Besides, it's hard for me to concentrate on my math when
Norma the booger picker is sitting right next to me. I never know
when she'll decide to pick and flick and sometimes she even eats 'em!"

RJ, just because you don't like doing math won't make it go away. Math is very important in life, and you need to learn how to do it the right way.

Do you ever ask your teacher for help?"

"No. It's just easier to do it my way. Besides, I don't want her to know that I don't get it."

"Well, RJ, I think she already knows."

"Last week in math, I asked Sam to help me.
But he got a ten when the answer was three.

Then my teacher got mad, 'cause we talked during math.
So she moved Sam away to the back of the class."

"RJ, you need to ask your teacher for help
when you don't understand something."

"I tried asking once, but we were taking a test.
So she said, 'RJ, sit down and just try your best.'

Another time I asked her when I didn't have a clue,
And she said, 'You're interrupting, RJ,
please wait 'til I'm through.'

When my teacher finished talking, math time was over,
So I never got the chance to ask her or show her."

"Could you have stayed in from recess to ask her how to do it?"

"I can't miss recess to do math!"

"You can't or you won't?" my mom asked.

"BOTH!"

The next morning my mom took me to school early so
we could look for my missing assignments in my desk.
It took us a while... but we found them... along
with a few other papers that were kinda,
sorta not quite all the way finished.

"RJ! This is ridiculous!" my mom said.

"You should always ask your teacher for help when you don't understand
something. You just need to figure out how and when to ask."

When you need to ask for help, this is what you should do:

Look right at the person whose attention you seek.

Ask, "Is now a good time for you to help me?"

Then clearly explain what it is that you need.

And remember to say, "Thanks for helping me!"

As soon as I got home from school, my mom looked at me and said, "RJ, life as you know it is going to change!"

(And it did!)

My mom gave me 20 minutes to eat my snack and have free time. Usually, I get at least an hour.

Then she sat with me at the kitchen table and together we worked on my half-way done assignments until they were all the way done. I had to sit there for like 46 years!

Before I went to bed that night, my dad came into my room to talk to me.

"RJ, Mom said you had to sit at the kitchen table for 46 years tonight getting your missing assignments done. You need to do a much better job of staying on task so you can finish your work and turn it in on time."

"That's exactly what my teacher says!"

"Well, RJ, when you start your assignments, you need to try harder to stay on task, so you will get farther.

If you keep on working until you are through, you'll just be amazed at what you're able to do!"

"But I don't like to do it
that way," I said.

"I like to do it my way,
So I don't have to do the same
thing over and over and over
again for a long, long, long time!"

"Well, son, your way isn't working out very well. Besides, if you stay on task, the 'over and over' part doesn't take that long.

"Yeah Dad, but it's hard to think about math when Norma the..."

"I know, I know, RJ. Mom told me."

"And sometimes during math, Rodney tries to
    burp the alphabet, and then everyone laughs, and then..."

"RJ, when I mow the lawn,
I get all of it done.
I don't stop in the middle,
even though it's not fun.

I work very hard
to finish my task,
'cause if I quit too soon,
we'll have crooked grass!

Your way works okay for a kid who is little,
but you're too big now, RJ, to stop in the middle...
even if Norma is picking her nose or Rodney is trying to burp the alphabet!"

The next day I went to school and
handed in all of my missing assignments
(about 46 years' worth)!

My teacher was so proud of me
that she did the HAPPY DANCE!

"RJ," she said, "I bet it feels great to be all caught up!"

"Now we need to figure out a way to help you stay caught up!

First of all, I want you to know that you can always ask me for help if you need it. If I can't help you right when you ask, I will make sure I find another time that works for both of us.

Now you need to do a better job of staying on task so you can finish your work and turn it in on time."

"That's exactly what my dad says, but I just don't like doing the same thing over and over and over for a long, long, long time! I just like to do it my way! Besides, Norma always..."

"I know, RJ, but your way just isn't working."

"When you need to stay on task you should:

Take a good look at
what it is you must do.

Focus on each step and
just think it through.

Don't let others interrupt
you or pull you away.

Keep working on through
and on task you will stay!

RJ, if you can stay on task, the 'over and over'
part won't take you as long!"

"I think from now on when it's time for you to work on your math, I'll let you go to the back of the room and sit in the VERB VILLA. You'll have a little bit more space to wiggle while you are working, and the other kids won't distract you as much."

So today during math, I tried doing things a different way.
I listened as closely as I could when my
teacher explained our assignment.

I understood just about all of it except for one little part, so I went up to her after, waited for the perfect time, and then asked her to help me. I remembered to tell her "thank you," just like my mom said.

Then I went to the back of the room and did my math
in the Verb Villa. I got all of it all the way done!!!

AND, I even understood it!!!

AND, the best part of all is, I didn't have to worry
about Norma's picking or Rodney's burping!

I looked at my teacher and thought,
  "Wow, could it be? Now this is a teacher who really gets me!

She's willing to help me each time that I ask,
  and she'll go out of her way to help keep me on task!

A new way of doing things is just what I need.
  And with the Verb Villa's help, I'm sure to succeed.

It feels great to be caught up and not be behind.
  Now my 'over and over' won't take so much time.

And hopefully,
  I won't have to spend another
    46-year night at the kitchen table!"

ASKING FOR HELP

🐘 Explain to your child that it is OK to ask for help. Asking for help shows that YOU are being responsible for yourself.

🐘 Make sure your child understands what it means to "get help." Getting help doesn't mean the other person "does it for you." It means the person "shows you how to do it." Asking for help with schoolwork is a way to add to your learning experience – not take from it.

🐘 Discuss with your child who and who not to go to when asking for help in various situations, both academic and nonacademic.

🐘 Explain to your child that there are good times to ask for help and not so good times to ask for help, depending on the situation.

🐘 Role-play scenarios that teach your child how to decide what kind of help is needed, who should be asked, when to ask, and what should be said. When learning HOW to ask for help, practice can make a big difference!

STAYING ON TASK

🐘 Make sure your directions are clear and understood. If you have your instructions written on the board, make sure that students make their own copies of the instructions for their desks. Also, make sure kids can tell you verbally what it is that you are asking them to do.

🐘 Make sure kids have everything they need in supplies at their desks before they start their assignments, so they don't have to leave their seats and wander around collecting what they need.

🐘 Make sure assignments are the appropriate length for the time allotted. Take work breaks as needed, and plan academic subjects in the AM. Limit screen time, and incorporate physical activity as much as you can throughout the day.

🐘 Remember, not every child works at the same rate. Set up a jigsaw puzzle or other activity in the back of the room, so that kids who finish their assignments early can have something to do that is both quiet and cooperative, and won't distract others.

🐘 Make sure your wiggly kids have room to "move" during work time without distracting others. Let them fiddle with focus squishies, or even sit on yoga balls. If they become too distracting to other students, set up a "VERB VILLA" in the back of your room. Remember: Working in the "VERB VILLA" is not a punishment, it is a learning opportunity.

🐘 Try strategically pairing kids up during work time. Sometimes it is easier to stay on task when you are working with another person. Kids can do wonders for each other through peer tutoring.

🐘 Tell kids what they "CAN" do and be as opposed to what they "CANNOT." Remember… you always get more bees with honey than you do with vinegar. Always offer more positive reinforcements than negative reinforcements. Instead of saying, "I hope you don't have another day, like yesterday," say, "Today is a brand new day, and I can't wait to see what you are going to do with it!"

🐘 Set up a point-reward system for staying on task and for finishing assignments. Remember: each child you teach has "What's in it for me?" tattooed to his/her forehead. Most kids have to be extrinsically motivated before they can teach themselves to become intrinsically motivated.

🐘 Use a timer. Most of the time, students who struggle with staying on task also struggle when it comes to time management. Kids often work better if they know there is a time limit in place.

🐘 Walk around your classroom and monitor what is going on. If you are on task with what your students are doing, they will have an easier time staying on task, too.

For more parenting information, visit

parenting.org
from **BOYS TOWN**

BEST ME I Can Be!
Titles!

Activity Guides
for Teachers
and Poster Sets
are also available!

BOYS TOWN® Press

BoysTownPress.org

ISBN 978-1-934490-20-4

ISBN 978-1-934490-23-5

ISBN 978-1-934490-35-8

ISBN 978-1-934490-37-2

ISBN 978-1-934490-25-9

ISBN 978-1-934490-27-3

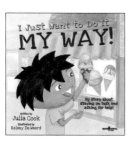
ISBN 978-1-934490-43-3

ISBN 978-1-934490-45-7

ISBN 978-1-934490-28-0

ISBN 978-1-934490-32-7

ISBN 978-1-934490-34-1

The Boys Town Education Model® and Common Sense Parenting®

The Boys Town Education Model is a school-based intervention model that emphasizes social skill instruction, classroom behavior management practices, and relationship building among students, teachers, administrators and other school staff. Many of the same techniques can also be found in the strategies that comprise Boys Town's Common Sense Parenting program.

A key component of the Education Model and Common Sense Parenting is a set of social skills for children that include listening, following instructions, accepting "no" for an answer, working with others, asking permission, and others. Teaching children social skills gives them the positive behaviors that contribute to harmony at home and success in school.

CONTACT BOYS TOWN

For more information on Boys Town, its Education Model, and Common Sense Parenting, visit BoysTown.org/educators, BoysTown.org/parents, or parenting.org, e-mail training@BoysTown.org, or call 1-800-545-5771.

For parenting and educational books and other resources, visit the Boys Town Press website at BoysTownPress.org, e-mail btpress@BoysTown.org, or call 1-800-282-6657.